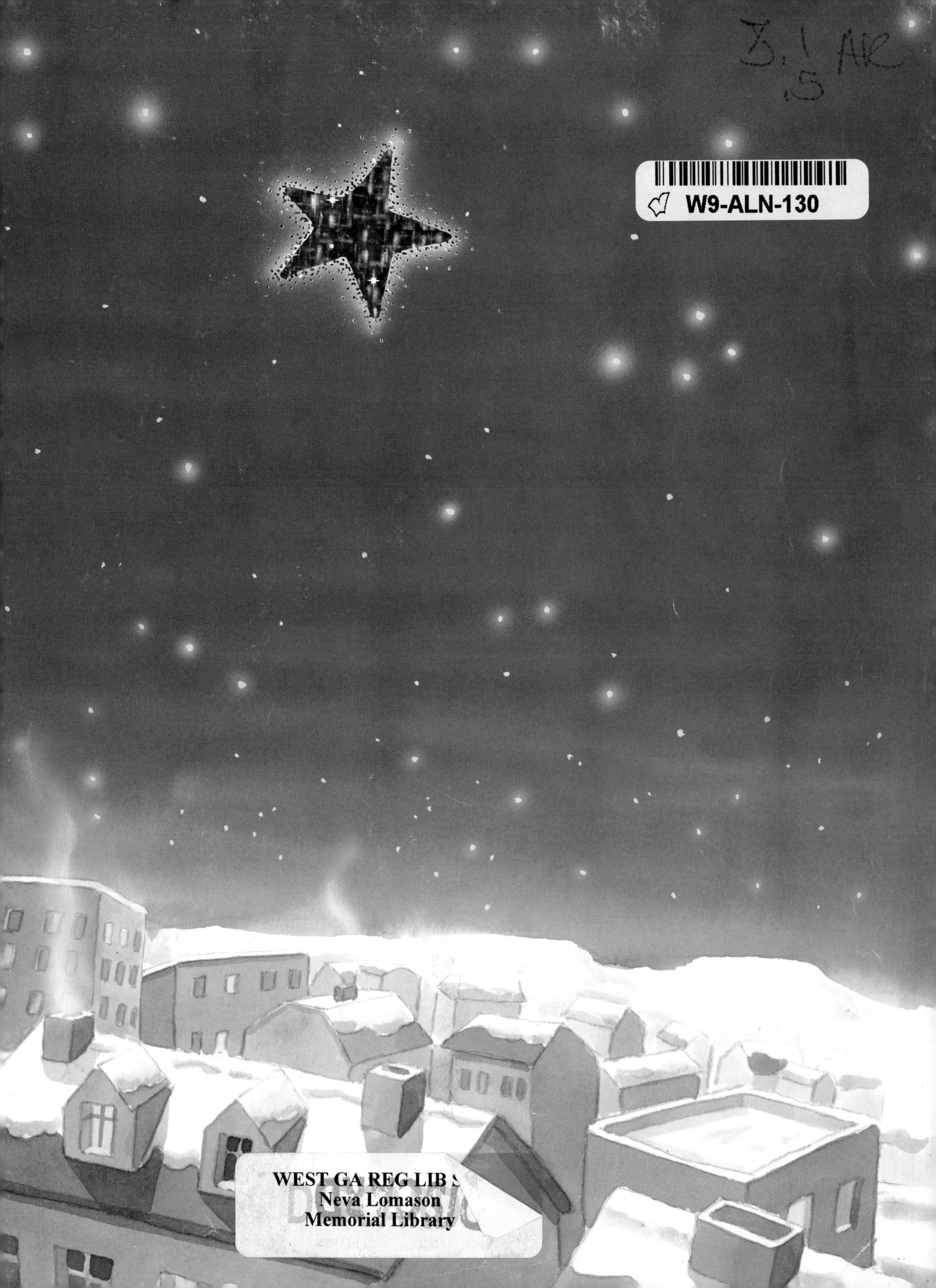

For you
and your own magic star

LITTLE TIGER PRESS
N16 W23390 Stoneridge Drive, Waukesha, WI 53188
First published in the United States 1999
Originally published in Germany 1998 by
Baumhaus Verlag, Frankfurt
Text and illustrations © 1998 Klaus Baumgart
English text © 1999 Magi Publications, London
All rights reserved
Library of Congress Cataloging-in-Publication-Data
Baumhaus, Klaus.
[Lauras Weihnachtsstern. English]
Laura's Christmas star / Klaus Baumgart.
p.   cm.
Summary : When her family's Christmas trip has to be cancelled,
Laura finds a way to create a special kind of magic for the holiday.
ISBN   1-888444-59-2   (hc)
[1. Christmas Fiction.]   I. Title.
PZ7.B3285Lar 1999 [E]—dc21 99-27986 CIP
Printed in Singapore
First American Edition
1 3 5 7 9 10 8 6 4 2

Laura's
Christmas Star

Klaus Baumgart

English text by Judy Waite

LITTLE TIGER PRESS

"Do you believe in magic?" asked Tommy, watching Laura pack her suitcase.

They were going to Aunt Martha's for Christmas this year. Laura smiled. It was a quiet, secret smile.

"Sometimes," she said.

"Aunt Martha says her Christmas tree looks magical," Tommy went on. "She says it's huge and sparkly and it glitters like a zillion stars. I can't *wait* to see it."

"Are you packed?" asked Mom, coming into the room. She gave them both a hug. "It's time for bed now. Otherwise you'll both be tired and grumpy on the journey to Aunt Martha's tomorrow."

Laura closed her eyes, letting pictures of a zillion glittery stars float into her thoughts.

"Is it morning now?" asked Tommy.

Laura opened one eye.

"We've only just gone to bed," she said. "Go back to sleep."

Laura closed her eyes again and thought of huge sparkly Christmas trees and colorful wrapping.

"Is it time to get up yet?" asked Tommy.

"No," said Laura. "It's still the middle of the night."

Ten minutes passed. It seemed like ten years to Tommy.

"Is it morning *now?*" asked Tommy, nudging Laura awake.

Laura opened both her eyes. She seemed to have slept a long time. "I think it must be," she said.

Laura and Tommy jumped up, pulled on their clothes, and ran into Mom and Dad's bedroom.

"It's not time to get up," groaned Mom, waking up. "Go back to bed!"

Laura and Tommy wandered back to their room, but they didn't go to bed. They sat by the window, staring out at the zillions of sparkly, glittering stars.

"Look!" cried Tommy, pointing. "That star's brighter than the others."

Laura smiled her secret smile. The bright star was her own, special, magic star. She had once rescued it when it had fallen from the sky. When it was better, she had set it free. Though it was now far away, she knew it was her friend.

At last morning came. Laura and Tommy helped Mom and Dad pack the car. Nearby on the sidewalk a man was selling Christmas trees. He waved at them and shouted "Merry Christmas!"

"We're going to spend Christmas at Aunt Martha's," Tommy shouted back. "She's got a Christmas tree that's huge and sparkly and glitters like a zillion stars."

At last they were off. The sky began to turn all gray and soft. It looked like it was going to snow.

As they reached the country, beautiful snowflakes began to drift down. Laura and Tommy pressed their noses against the car window and watched them cover the earth like icing on a Christmas cake.

Suddenly the car began to rattle. It began to cough.

"It sounds like it's got a bad cold," said Laura.

"It sounds like it's broken down," said Mom.

Everyone got out, and Dad opened up the hood. He pulled at some wires, but he didn't get the car started.

Everyone climbed back into the car and waited for
the repairman to arrive. It grew colder and colder, and
everyone huddled together to keep warm. Dad tried
singing Christmas songs and telling jokes, but the songs
sounded flat, and the jokes weren't funny.

"I'll tell you a story," said Laura. "It's about a magic
Christmas star that saves everybody."

But as she started, Tommy began to cry. "There's no
such thing as magic," he whispered sadly. "We'll never
get to Aunt Martha's now. I'll never see her huge sparkly
Christmas tree that glitters like a zillion stars."

By the time the repairman
had fixed the car, it was too late to go to Aunt Martha's.
Tommy tried not to cry as Dad drove back home and they
carried their suitcases into the house.

Tommy stayed sad as the daylight faded and the night crept back into the sky.

"I wish I could do something to make Tommy happy again," Laura whispered. She looked out of her bedroom, and her special star appeared. It shone down at her, as if it understood Tommy's sadness.

The man who had been selling Christmas trees was long gone, but suddenly Laura noticed that he had left behind a little tree. It lay in the snow looking ragged and battered and very lonely. "I'll get it for Tommy," Laura cried. "Maybe it will cheer him up."

Laura ran outside to where the little
tree was lying. "Come indoors with me,"
she said. "You look awfully lonely out
here on your own."

Laura carried the tree into the house.

"Thanks for getting it," said Tommy sadly. "It's a nice little tree. But it's not very sparkly, is it? It's not very glittery."

Laura looked at the tree. Tommy was right. It could never be like the magical tree Aunt Martha had promised them.

Laura went upstairs to sit by her window. At least she could tell her star how helpless she felt. It always listened to her and understood. But as she looked into the night sky, she gasped with horror. Her special star had disappeared!

Now Laura was as sad as Tommy. There wasn't much
to feel happy about now that she had lost a special friend.
And maybe Tommy was right. Maybe there was no such
thing as magic after all.

Suddenly, she heard Dad calling to them. "Laura,
Tommy, come here quickly!"

Puzzled, the two children trailed downstairs.

"Look!" gasped Mom, as they all stood by the
living-room door.

Laura and Tommy looked. They couldn't believe what
they were seeing.

"It's *wonderful!*" cried Tommy, turning to Laura with
shining eyes. "But how could it have happened?"

Laura smiled her quiet, secret smile.
She knew, of course. "It must be magic,"
she said.